This

belongs to:

....

....

The Fireless Dragon

and other stories

Written by
NICOLA BAXTER

Illustrated by
ANDREW WARRINGTON

This is a Parragon Book
This edition published in 2002

Parragon
Queen Street House
4 Queen Street
Bath BA1 1HE, UK

Copyright © Parragon 2000

ISBN 0-75259-498-2

Produced for Parragon by
Nicola Baxter

Designed by Amanda Hawkes
Cover designed by Gemma Hornsby
Cover illustrated by Andrew Everitt- Stewart
Additional illustrations by Richard Duszczak

Printed in Italy

Contents

The Fireless Dragon   7

The Tiniest Dragon   29

The Most Dangerous Dragon   51

Treasure Trouble   77

The Flightless Dragon   99

The Dragon's Egg   123

The Fireless Dragon

Idon't know if you have ever thought about the extraordinary way in which dragons breathe fire. Everyone knows they do it, but scientists have never been able to get close enough to one to find out exactly how it works. For one thing, why don't dragons singe their own nostrils? The firefighting forces of the world would dearly like to find out. It could save them a fortune on fire-proof suits.

Another good question that is often asked concerns baby dragons. As you know, dragons hatch from eggs—big eggs. Like most babies, they don't actually start breathing until they are out in the world. In any case, breathing fire *inside* an egg is asking for trouble. So how do they start? Luckily, this is one subject I can give you the facts about, as all is revealed in the story of young Albertus, the fireless, fearless dragon.

Most dragons only lay one egg at a time. If you could see the size of those eggs, you would know why. Occasionally, they lay two. Very rarely, two baby dragons hatch from the same egg.

What happened to Maralu, the mother of young Albertus, is very rare indeed. First of all, she laid two eggs—a feat in itself. Like most dragons, she didn't sit on them or anything, but she made sure they were in a warm, dry cave, where mountaineers wouldn't stick pick-axes into them and geologists wouldn't carry them off. Dragon eggs, you see, look very much like large boulders. I once saw one in a very posh person's garden. It had been carried there from overseas and it looked very fine. I wondered very much what would happen when it hatched!

Hatching, like many things with dragons, takes years and years. Most dragon mothers sleep through this time, conserving their strength for the years ahead when they will have to look after one or more difficult little dragons.

Maralu's two eggs lay snugly in her cave, next to the sleeping mother, for over ten years. Then, one fine spring morning, Maralu woke up feeling a little hungry. She dashed off at once and luckily found a couple of maidens wandering aimlessly in a meadow nearby. We needn't go into the details. It is enough to say that Maralu had a good breakfast and the maidens wander no more.

Back in the cave, Maralu prowled around her eggs. She had a feeling that something was about to happen and she was right. The largest egg began first. It started to rock, ever so gently.

Under Maralu's watchful eyes, the egg rocked faster and faster, until it bashed into the smaller egg. Like a chain reaction, this egg, too, began to rock. Soon both eggs were jiggling about in a completely extraordinary way. They juddered and they shuddered. They jiggled and they joggled. Then, very suddenly, the largest egg went *crack!* with tremendous force. Even Maralu jumped back in alarm.

A large piece of shell fell away from the top of the hatching egg. Out of the hole popped a cheeky little face.

Maralu hurried across to her baby. He looked adorable. But Maralu's shocks were not over. Just as she was about to lift him out of the egg, another little face popped up beside him. This one was even more adorable than the first, and it was a girl. Maralu's heart went thuddedy-dong. (Sorry, I haven't told you about dragon heartbeats. The point is, she was delighted.)

Maralu helped her two little ones out of the egg. They were perfect. They had all their little claws and scales, just as they should. They were not, of course, breathing fire. Maralu bent down and very, very gently blew into their tiny noses. It was a bit like lighting the gas. At once, little flickering flames and puffs of smoke came out. Two more little dragons were breathing fire and not scorching their nostrils at all.

Maralu was so delighted with her little ones and the surprise of having twins that she didn't notice what was happening to the other egg for an hour or two. When she did look up, she saw that it was still rocking, but the rocking was becoming less vigorous. It was as if the little creature inside was finding it just too exhausting to crack his egg. Even as Maralu watched, the rocking stopped completely. The egg sat there and just quivered ever so slightly.

Maralu was concerned. She knew that being able to get out of an egg was a good first test for a young dragon. Little ones who couldn't manage that were likely to have a difficult life. Sometimes, so the old dragons said, it was kinder to leave an unhatched egg and let nature take its course. But Maralu, filled with warm feelings for her new family, couldn't do that. She hurried forward and used her claws to break open the egg. *Crack!* The shell fell apart, leaving a little dragon body panting on the floor of the cave.

This little dragon was certainly not as vigorous and robust as the other two, who were already jumping up and down around the cave and playing leaptail over their mother. But the new little one looked up at Maralu and gave a grateful little smile. The dragon mother's heart melted. She scooped the baby up into her arms and took him off to a corner of the cave where the other two wouldn't jump on him.

The new baby soon began to look better. He stretched and yawned. Then he sat up and began to take an interest in what was going on around him. Maralu was delighted. He looked like a clever little chap. If he wasn't as big and strong as her other children, it didn't matter. Maralu bent down and blew gently into the little one's nose to light his flames.

Nothing happened.

She blew again.

Still nothing.

A little frightened now, Maralu blew harder still.

"Ouch!" said the little dragon.

Maralu tried to think reassuring thoughts. She would try again in a couple of hours, when the little one was on his feet. It would be okay. Still, she watched her son anxiously as he hopped over to play with his brother and sister.

Maralu had had a long time to think about names for her little ones. Two boys'

names and two girls' names (as she only knew that there would be two babies, not three) were ready and waiting. Maralu called the twins Magnus and Agnes. The smallest baby was called Albertus.

Over the next few days, Maralu tried several times to light Albertus's flames. It was no good. His little nose grew sore at her attempts. In the end, it seemed cruel to keep trying, but Maralu was deeply worried.

How would her son cope when it was time for him to go out and find his own maidens to munch? No one, surely, would run screaming from a dragon with no fire and smoke belching from his nostrils?

As the little dragons grew up, they turned out to have different characters and strengths. Agnes was strong and fierce. She chased little mice and frogs all over the mountainside when she was still quite small—and she caught quite a lot of them. Magnus was quieter and more timid. He didn't chase anything at all until he suddenly found that with his long legs he was even faster than Agnes. Then he tore around at high speed. He didn't catch anything, but Maralu was sure that his burst of speed would stand him in good stead.

Albertus was different. He wasn't very strong and he wasn't very fierce. He couldn't run fast enough to catch anything, but he was incredibly brave. When he was still very little, he saved his whole family from a mountain lion—by roaring.

"Well, I didn't know what else to do," Albertus explained later. "He was just standing there, looking at us, and he was much fiercer than us, so I simply charged towards him and roared. I was hoping he would run away. I don't know what I would have done if he hadn't."

"But he did," said Magnus with admiration. "You frightened *him*. It was brilliant, Bert."

"Don't call him that," said Maralu sharply. "It's not dignified. Always remember, my dears, that dragons have a long and distinguished history. We have to uphold the honour of our ancestors."

None of the children had the first idea what she was talking about, but they said, "Yes, Mamma," and trotted off to play as usual.

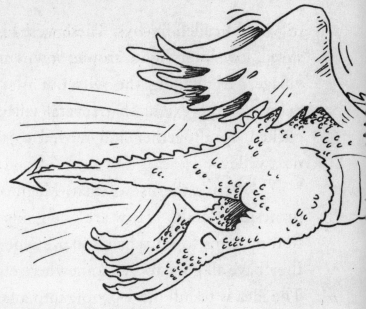

Teenage dragons are just as difficult as teenagers of any other species. Poor Maralu had a terrible time restraining Agnes' tendency to eat anything that moved (including hay wagons, which did her digestion no good at all). It was just as difficult trying to persuade Magnus to keep still for a moment. When he discovered his wings, Magnus found another area in which he could be speedy. He specialized in what he called fly-bys. These were high speed, low-level flights around towns and villages, frightening the wits out of the people to the extent that several villages packed up altogether and moved to the next valley.

"What's the use of that, Magnus?" protested Maralu. "How are you going to find maidens to eat when you are older if they have all gone to live somewhere else? The idea is to lull these people into a false sense of security by sleeping for a few years, then dash out and make a raid when you feel really hungry. It's worked well for dragons for hundreds of years. Now you have everyone so jittery they don't let their maidens out of their sight. Last month I had to make do with sheep, and it's not the same at all. I know all this is just boyish high spirits, but you are old enough now to be more responsible."

"Yes, Mamma," said Magnus, but he didn't mean it. A few days later, however, he caught his claws in a washing-line and almost came to a very nasty end on a furious farmer's wife's pitchfork. After that, he calmed down a good deal.

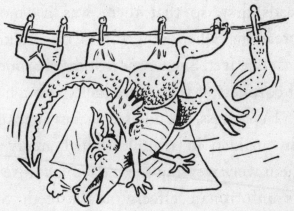

At last the day came when Maralu had only one more thing to teach her babies. Then they would have to go off and find caves of their own.

"Agnes, Magnus, Albertus," she said, "today I will teach you the art of catching and eating maidens. Then you will be grown-ups and can look after yourselves. Now listen carefully."

Maralu explained about the great importance of surprise, the use of smoke and fire in quelling excessive struggling and screaming, the advisability of eating heads first, so that there was no more screaming when you got to the trickier bits, like feet. She warned of the sharpness of coronets, if they were lucky enough to find a princess. She advised against attacking any maiden in armour (which many of them were wearing these days) because of its unfortunate effects on the teeth. She explained that it was simply not done to eat children or old ladies, however hungry you were, but any female between twenty and forty-five was fair game. The rules had been relaxed a lot since the olden days. She warned against feelings of mercy and sympathy.

"It's a slippery slope," she said. "You let one go and you'll start doing it all the time. Everyone knows that dragons eat maidens. It's part of nature. You can't interfere with nature. Now, let's go out and put all this theory into practice."

The four dragons set off together, down to the watermeadows beside the river. There were quite often maidens mooning about down there, picking flowers or combing their hair.

By chance, conditions were perfect. Three perfectly edible maidens were wandering about separately in the water-meadows, which at this time of year were far from watery. Wildflowers bloomed among the grasses. It was an idyllic picture.

"Now," hissed Maralu, "remember, if you do enough with the fire and flames, there won't *be* any screaming. Terrify them enough, and they'll drop down in a faint. Maidens do that sort of thing. Then everything is much easier for everyone. As for you, Albertus, I'm afraid you'll just have to try your roaring trick, but I'm very much afraid that you may have to go without maidens. Give it a try, though. Some of those maidens are frightened by spiders and worms. A great big dragon might just be terrifying enough without flames and smoke."

The three young dragons trotted off obediently. Then, just as the first maiden noticed them coming, they leapt into action. Magnus and Agnes got to their maidens first, of course. They did the full fire and smoke thing, but they did it a little too vigorously. In seconds, the whole meadow of dryish grass and flowers was alight. The maidens screamed and ran towards the river, hurling themselves in with a great splash. The dragons hopped about in frustration. Their nostrils may be fireproof, but their toes are not.

Dragons, of course, hate water. They live in mortal dread of putting their flames out. Albertus, however, did not. He slithered into the water with the grace of an over-sized otter and had eaten the three maidens before his brother and sister had stopped hopping up and down.

After that, Maralu had no fears for her youngest child. He was brave. He was resourceful. He was clever. The fact that he wasn't fire-breathing hardly seemed to matter. Maralu gave a huge sigh of relief (setting several trees alight) and turned her attention to her more unruly twins. Clearly, more work was necessary *there*.

The Tiniest Dragon

Edward was a boy who didn't believe anything he was told. He always had to see for himself. It was partly because he was pretty clever and from an early age had realized that grown-ups say some very silly things to children.

"Here comes the big orange plane," his mother used to coo, swooping a large spoonful of carrots towards his mouth when he was a toddler. Edward looked at her in disgust. "It isn't," he said, and shut

his mouth firmly.

"Oh Edward! You're hurting poor Mr. Bear," his father used to say, when Edward tried out his new plastic hammer on Mr. Bear's nose.

"He isn't alive, you know," said Edward coldly.

When Edward was older, things became even more difficult. At Grandma's birthday party, when she giggled and told him she was thirty-nine, Edward's "You've got to be joking!" rather spoilt the festive atmosphere.

Later, at school, Edward's teachers found him hard work. He always wanted proof of anything they said, and that could be difficult.

"How do you know there's nothing growing on the moon?" he asked. "Have you ever been there?"

"No, of course not," replied the teacher, "but other people have. Their reports say that there is nothing at all growing on the moon."

"People often don't tell the truth," said Edward grimly. "How do you know you can trust them?"

"You'll just have to take my word for it, Edward," replied his teacher. "Now we must move on."

Edward's questions, she knew from experience, could take up the whole lesson. It was very difficult.

As time went on, Edward found there were not many subjects that he felt happy about. Maths was fine. He could work out the problems and feel confident that everything was true—and provable. Music was okay, too. He could hear with his own ears if something sounded right. History and geography were minefields until a new teacher explained to him one day about *evidence*. After that, Edward began to enjoy the idea of using real things to show what was true. He was upset when Grandma refused to lend him her birth certificate to back up his family history project, but Granddad was more helpful.

"Of course, he's much older than me," said Grandma.

The subject that Edward found most difficult was English. Time and again, he was asked to make up a story about something

"But what's the point?" asked Edward.

"It helps your imagination to grow," said one teacher. "I'm sure you make up lots of wonderful stories in your head, Edward. We just want to hear some of them."

"No, I don't," said the boy. "Why would I want to do that? It wouldn't be true. You can't trust made-up things."

"Well, in a way you're right," replied the teacher, "but you can enjoy them. And sometimes they're true in other ways. If you read a story about a boy being afraid of a ghost, for example, it doesn't mean that there really are ghosts or that there really was a boy who was afraid of them. It means that people are often afraid of things they don't really understand. That's true, even if the story isn't, do you see?"

Edward looked unconvinced. "I'll write a diary instead," he said. "It will be a sort of story, but it will be true."

The teacher sighed and agreed.

One term, Mrs. Martin the teacher announced that instead of writing lots of different stories, each pupil would write one long story, like a proper book. They would write a chapter each week. At the end, a real author, who lived nearby, would come and read the books and award prizes for the most imaginative. All the children were very excited—except one, of course.

"I don't know why I have to bother," he said. "Mine isn't going to be imaginative at all. I'm going to write a diary again."

"Well, if that is what you feel happy doing, that will be fine," said his teacher, but it didn't make *her* feel happy. For the past year she had read dozens of "stories" from Edward, all of them in diary form, and they were, frankly, desperately boring.

"Today I got up at seven thirty. I had cereal and an orange for breakfast. It was raining when I set off for school, so I wore my raincoat. I looked at my gauge and saw that two centimetres of rain had fallen overnight. I told Mrs. Martin at school, but she didn't seem interested. James Prothero stole my pencil. We had cheese salad and apple pie for lunch. I got A$^+$ for my maths homework. It was still raining when I went home."

Mrs. Martin thought of having to read a whole book full of this kind of thing and shuddered, but there was no alternative. Edward would only write about things he knew were true, and that was the end of it.

But Edward's life was about to change in the most extraordinary way. That evening, after he had eaten his supper (and recorded every mouthful in his new "story" diary), Edward sat down at the desk in his room to do his homework. It was maths, which he enjoyed, so it was some time before he noticed little puffs of smoke coming from his pencil-case.

Edward looked down at it in horror. He had learnt about fire safety in school. His pencils must be on fire! He knew he shouldn't open the zip, in case the fire spread, so he ran into the bathroom, filled a tumbler with water, and threw it over the pencil-case, first moving his maths homework well out of the way. The smoke stopped at once, but something even odder happened. The pencil-case began to splutter.

Edward watched it in amazement. With each splutter (and what sounded very like a cough) the pencil-case gave a little jump. Summing up the possibilities in his mind, Edward could come to only one conclusion. There was something (very small) inside.

The more he thought about it, the surer Edward became that what was inside his pencil-case must be a mouse. It could have crept in at school and been chewing his pencils ever since. Maybe it wasn't smoke he had seen. Maybe it was puffs of sawdust or something like that. Edward didn't much like the idea of a mouse running about in his bedroom, so he carried the dripping case carefully into the bathroom, shut the door firmly (and locked it), and put the jiggling pencil-case down in the sink. Then, very, very slowly, he pulled back the zip.

It wasn't a mouse, although it was about that size. Mice, Edward knew, are not green and orange with wings. It must, he thought, be a bat—some kind of fruit-eating bat from a tropical country. But just as Edward was thinking of going back to his room to look up the creature in his nature encyclopedia, the animal gave a final splutter and began to smoke. I don't mean that it had a cigarette or anything horrible like that. I mean that little puffs of smoke began coming out of its nose.

Edward's mind was racing. He seemed to remember some story from school about a legend that salamanders live in fires. But salamanders didn't have wings, he knew. And anyway, that was just a story. It wasn't *true*. It was because salamanders often live in dead logs, and when these are thrown on to a fire, they run out. This little creature wasn't running anywhere. It looked perfectly happy. Edward hurried out of the bathroom, shutting the door carefully behind him, and retrieved his magnifying glass from his room. Locked safely in the bathroom again, he approached the creature once more. This time, he could make a proper, scientific identification.

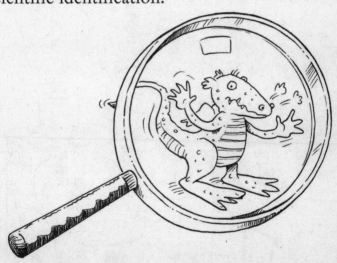

It was a while before Edward could believe what his eyes were telling him. Using the magnifying glass, he could see that not only smoke but tiny flames were coming from the creature's nostrils. He could see that the green and orange skin was made up of tiny scales. He could see that it had a long tail with a forked bit on the end. In short, he could see that the tiny animal sitting quietly in the sink was not a mouse, or a fruit-bat, or a salamander. It was a dragon.

You know, and I know, and Edward knew that dragons are not *real*, like cows and pigs are real. They are imaginary, like fairies and goblins and unicorns. But Edward also knew that one of these entirely imaginary creatures was sitting in his bathroom sink. He needed to do some serious thinking—and fast!

You or I might have been puzzled about the whole thing. So puzzled that our brains refused to take in what we were seeing or to think slowly and sensibly about it afterwards. Edward, after a couple of minutes, found that the situation was surprisingly simple. How, he reasoned, did he know that there were no such things as dragons? He knew because books and teachers had told him so. Did he believe everything that he read in books or was told by teachers? No! Did he believe things he could see to be true with his own eyes? Definitely! There was no question about it. There was a tiny dragon in his bathroom. The only problem now was deciding what to do next.

"I wish," said Edward, thinking out loud, "that I knew what dragons like to eat. At least, I think that big dragons like to eat people, but what could this one manage?" He peered again at the creature.

"Mmmmnnnng," said the dragon, with its mouth full. Clearly hungry, the dragon had answered the question itself by tucking into the soap. Although Edward was doubtful whether this was a nutritious meal for any reptile, the dragon itself seemed perfectly happy. Half a bar disappeared before it sat down with what sounded very like a burp. Edward, thinking that the creature must now be thirsty, turned on the cold tap so that just a little trickle came out of it.

At once, a tiny screeching came from the sink, and the dragon started to hop about in an agitated way. Edward bent down. It wasn't screeching. The dragon was talking, but in a very, very tiny voice.

"Turn it off! Turn it off!" it was squeaking. "Don't you know anything? Turn it off!"

Edward did as he was told. Then he leaned down again and asked, "Why?"

"Dragons *hate* water!" squealed the dragon. "It puts our flames out! And they're *so* difficult to light again. Which reminds me…"

"Oh," Edward knew what was coming. "I'm sorry about that," he said, "throwing the water over you, I mean. I thought my pencil-case was on fire."

"That was pretty silly," commented the dragon. "What on earth made you think that?"

"The smoke," said Edward sharply. He didn't take kindly to being told he was silly by a creature not much bigger than his nose. "*Your* smoke," he pointed out.

"Ah, well, I suppose I can see your point," said the dragon. "That could have been the explanation. But didn't it occur to you that it might be a dragon?"

"Of course not," replied Edward. "I didn't know dragons existed."

"Didn't know they existed? Our publicity of late has been shockingly bad," sighed the dragon. "But I know for a fact that there are dozens of children's stories with dragons in them. How could you possibly not know? Can't you read?"

"Of course I can!" Edward was even more indignant. "But those stories are made up. The things in them aren't true, you know."

"Really?" There was deep sarcasm in the dragon's tone. "So how do you explain me, then?"

Edward couldn't.

The dragon stayed with Edward for almost two months. He seemed to appear at odd times, but never when anyone else was around. It didn't occur to Edward not to record his conversations with the dragon in his story-diary.

Those two months changed Edward's life. He had to think again about many things, such as whether you could believe what you read in books and what it really meant to say that something was true. He began to notice things he had never noticed before, such as the way that clouds sometimes looked like dragons and that there seemed to be a man smiling in the moon. He knew that the clouds weren't dragons and there was no man in the moon, but he understood now that it could be fun to think about things that only *seemed* to be true. His family, his teachers and his friends gradually found him much, much easier to be around. He liked them better, too.

Even so, Edward was amazed when his diary was chosen as "the story showing the most imagination" at the end of term. He was even more amazed by the pleasure that his success seemed to give everyone else. It was really nice. He liked it so much that he didn't notice until the next day that the dragon had gone—completely.

Edward searched for a long time. He even hunted in those places you'd rather not investigate, such as the darkest corners of the bathroom and inside his brother's trainers. There was no sign of the dragon.

For several weeks, Edward felt sure that from the corner of his eye he caught sight of little flickering flames and puffs of smoke. But however fast he turned around, they were never really there.

So the dragon had disappeared for ever. Nowadays, Edward is even happy about that. And on cold, frosty mornings, when his breath looks like little puffs of smoke, he wears a secret smile.

The Most Dangerous Dragon

Sometimes, when a cold wind whistled around the turrets of the castle, and the hunting dogs crowded close to the great fire, old Duncan Dobetter told stories to the youngsters of the court. His favourite subject was … dragons.

"As you know, a dragon is always dangerous," Duncan would say, pulling his cloak closer about his shoulders, "but the dragon you should truly fear is the most dangerous dragon of all. He is the invisible dragon. He could be with us now, here in this hall, and we would never know until it was TOO LATE!"

Stefan Stinkle listened with interest. He had long been trying to think of a way of making his mark in the world. Dragon-slaying seemed a good option. Instant fame and certain wealth had a great deal of appeal. But did old Duncan know what he was talking about? Had he, for example, ever come face to face with a dragon himself?

"Let me tell you, young Stinkle," cried Duncan, "I've met more dragons than you've had hot flagons, which I hope at your age isn't very many. I'll tell you a story that will make your hair stand on end."

Stefan smirked. "Go on then," he said.

Duncan settled down near the fire and beckoned the youngsters, including Stefan, to join him. When he spoke, his voice was dark and mysterious.

"When I was young," he said, "and you can wipe that expression off your face right away, young Stinkle—I *was* young once—my grandmother warned me that in every generation of our family at least one son was lost to a dragon. 'It has been that way with the Dobetters,' she said, 'since the beginning of time, and it will be that way for ever. I thought it was only fair to warn you, young Duncan, that your days are numbered.'"

"But why did it have to be you?" asked one of the lads. "Couldn't it have been a brother or a cousin?"

"It could," said Duncan, "if I had had any brothers or male cousins. But I didn't. I had seven sisters myself and more girl cousins than I could count. There were only two options. Either my parents had more children, or I met my doom."

"And did they?" Even Stefan Stinkle was getting interested. He had six sisters himself and experienced a certain fellow feeling for old Duncan.

"Yes, they did," said the old man. "They had four more children ... and they were all girls. Since it seemed that I would one day die at the claws of a dragon, I decided to find out all I could about the dreaded creature. I hoped that I would be able to use my wits to stave off the evil hour for as long as possible. I became, in a remarkably short time, an expert on the habits and habitats of every kind of dragon known to humankind. It was quite fascinating."

"Why?" asked Stefan, thinking of his future career. "What is there to know?"

"Ah," old Duncan took another swig from his goblet. "There is a very great deal to know. Could you tell me, for example, how dragons are born?"

"Born? They're not born!" scoffed Stefan. "They just *are* like mountains and music. Dragons are always hundreds of years old, aren't they?"

"Dragons who bother humans are usually hundreds of years old, yes," said Duncan, "but all dragons were young once. They hatch out of eggs, deep in the mountains."

"I've never heard of a dragon's egg," said another listener. "Why hasn't anyone ever seen one?"

"Because they are grey, like rocks, and very big. You have probably all seen them, but they just look like big, grey boulders to you."

The boys shuddered.

"How big are baby dragons?" they asked, frowning.

"About as big as a cow," replied the dragon expert. "But they are very shy. Their mothers keep them deep inside a cosy cave until they are ready to start rampaging about the countryside."

"What do they eat, deep inside the cave?" asked Stefan. He wasn't sure he believed any of this.

"Anyone their mother brings back from her hunting trips," replied Duncan.

"*Anyone?* But don't they eat cows and sheep and rabbits and things, too?" asked Marku, the budding naturalist.

"Only if they are very hungry," said Duncan. "Humans are their preferred food. They particularly like people with red hair and long noses. You were saying, Stinkle?"

"Nothing," said Stefan, pulling down his helmet.

"I want to hear more of the story," said a boy. "You said that you had met dragons. What happened?"

"The very first dragon that I met was that very dangerous kind I mentioned at the beginning. He was invisible, but absolutely deadly."

"If he was invisible, how did you know he was there?" Stefan was still unimpressed.

"Believe me, Stinkle, when you are in the presence of a dragon, *you know*. At least, you know if you have your wits about you. It happened like this. I was walking through the woods one day when I began to notice a smell of burning. The air felt warmer, too, although the day was cold and the leaves of the trees shut out the sun. As I walked on, I noticed that patches of leaves and bits of tree trunks were black, as if they had been scorched. I should have known the truth then, but I didn't have the sense to see it. I just kept on walking."

"Could you hear the dragon?"

"No, the woods were strangely silent. That should have warned me, but it didn't. Not a single bird sang in the branches. There were no squirrels or little woodland creatures of any kind. I walked on in the eerie silence … into a thick and suffocating fog."

"A fog? Like the one that forms in the valley every morning?" asked one lad.

"Exactly like that," replied Duncan with a smile. "This fog swirled around me in a strange way. I kept thinking I could glimpse shapes and shadows on the path, but there was never anything there. And the fog was warm, too, not cold and clammy like most mists. It was the breath of the dragon, you see, curling around the trees and surrounding me. I still didn't know that it was a dragon, but I began to be very frightened. For one thing, I knew that I was completely lost."

"You should have marked the trees," said Stefan. "Everyone knows that's what you should do if you can't find your way."

"Well, perhaps you are right," said Duncan, "but I've never seen how that could help. It wouldn't stop you walking in a circle, it would just mean that you would know if you were … walking in a circle, I mean. Anyway, I didn't do it, so it's neither here nor there. What I did do, which was a big mistake, was to call out for help."

"That's what I would have done," said one of the listeners, loyally.

"Thank you, Clarence. It did seem a good idea at the time. And only a few seconds later it seemed as if help had come. An old man appeared out of the fog, wearing a thick grey cloak with a hood over his eyes. One moment he wasn't there. The next, he sort of formed himself out of a thicker area of fog. At least, that's what it seemed like, but the light can play strange tricks with your eyes."

"But wasn't it spooky, if you couldn't see his face?" Clarence wasn't the bravest lad in the castle.

"I didn't think of that then," Duncan explained. "I was just so glad to see another human soul. I ran towards him shouting out with delight. It was only when I reached him, and he raised his hooded head, that I saw his ghastly face."

"What was it like?" All the lads asked together.

"My words may have been a little misleading," said Duncan slowly, taking another drink from his goblet. "What was really terrifying was that there was no face. The figure in the dark robes had an even darker void where his face should have been."

"Did you run?" asked Clarence.

"My feet were rooted to the spot. Even if I had wanted to escape, my legs refused to move. And in any case, it didn't matter. In a second or two, the horrible figure in front of me began to dissolve into the mist. It seemed to swirl for a moment and then was gone."

"What a relief!" said Marku.

"In a way," replied Duncan, gazing into the dying embers of the fire, "but I suddenly felt more alone than I had ever

been in my life. And what happened next was even more frightening."

He sipped again from his goblet.

"Go on! Go on!" The boys were desperate to know what had happened.

"The mist began to thicken," said Duncan, holding one hand after another out to the fire as though he felt a chill deep in his bones. "And it suddenly became very, very hot. I could feel a burning on my neck and face as the swirling air licked at it."

"It was the dragon!" cried Clarence.

"Yes, but I still didn't know that. I only knew that I was absolutely terrified and that my thoughts were whirling so fast in my head that I couldn't think of a single sensible thing to do. In fact, I was a young lad then, so I'm not ashamed to tell you that tears were streaming down my face as I stood there."

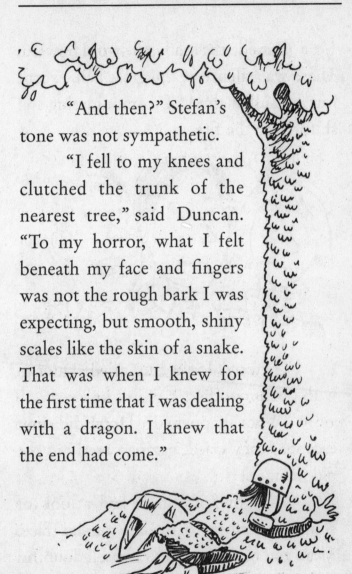

"And then?" Stefan's tone was not sympathetic.

"I fell to my knees and clutched the trunk of the nearest tree," said Duncan. "To my horror, what I felt beneath my face and fingers was not the rough bark I was expecting, but smooth, shiny scales like the skin of a snake. That was when I knew for the first time that I was dealing with a dragon. I knew that the end had come."

Outside the castle, the wind howled. There was silence in the great hall, except for the sullen thud of a smouldering log shifting on the fire.

The boys looked up at old Duncan with open mouths.

"What happened? How did you escape?" they cried, gazing eagerly at the old man.

Only Stefan Stinkle had a look of something close to disdain on his face. More and more, he found himself doubtful about Duncan Dobetter's story. Worse still, he began to wonder if he had been right to consider a dragon-slaying career. Clearly, Duncan had escaped from the encounter he was now describing. And, if what he had said before was to be believed, it was not the only time he had met a dragon and survived. If a man like Duncan Dobetter—not particularly clever, or brave, or strong—could meet dozens of dragons and survive, it must be pretty easy. And something that anyone could do would never bring in the fame and riches that Stefan had planned for himself. As these things passed through his mind, he felt Duncan's eyes upon him, a peculiar expression on his aged face.

Duncan leaned down to fill his goblet from the flagon standing near the hearth. It was empty.

"Stefan," he said mildly, "my old throat is parched. I must have some more of the cook's devilish brew before I go on. Will you go down to the kitchens and fill the flagon for me?"

"Oh, why me?" whined Stefan at once. "Why can't one of the others go?" But something in the old man's face stopped him. Picking up the empty vessel, he set off reluctantly for the kitchens far below in the depths of the castle.

Now, I expect you know very well that medieval castles were not the most comfortable of places. They were dark, cold and draughty. There was no glass in the tiny slit-like windows. You either froze in the passages and stairways or almost suffocated in the smoke of the rooms with fires. The only positive thing to be said for living in a castle was that it was a whole lot better than sleeping under a hedge, which was the fate of most of the peasants living round about.

Stefan Stinkle's mind wasn't on peasants as he made his way down the steep, circular stone stairs. The treads were worn by many feet, and the flaming torches that burned on the walls were few and far between. It was hard enough to keep your footing at the best of times, but with freezing draughts whistling around your ears and a flagon pressed to your chest, it was harder than usual.

The flickering torches made weird shadows jump and twist on the walls. Stefan felt himself shivering, and not only from the cold. Who could know what was lurking around the next curve? Or what was creeping down the stairs behind him?

Never had Stefan been so glad to reach the warmth and noise of the kitchens, a place he usually hated. They were filled with the steamy smells of cooking food, cooling food and, in the darkest corners, rotting food. The cook, too, a huge man with hands like shovels, dressed in a greasy robe, was terrifying at the best of times. Tonight, though, he looked reassuringly normal and human.

Stefan filled the flagon and only turned once more towards the stairs with the greatest reluctance.

It was even worse going up than coming down. The flagon was heavier, and Stefan soon found himself panting as he climbed the uneven steps. His breathing sounded unnaturally loud in his ears. Once again he began to have strange fears.

Was that a sound, lower than the howling of the wind, sharper than his ragged breaths, just above in the darkness? Surely there had been more light on the way down? By the time Stefan rounded the final curve and saw ahead of him the open doorway of the great hall, he had worked himself up into a real panic. His mouth felt dry and his legs trembled.

His footsteps quickened as he saw the flickering orange light from the fire through the doorway. He had never felt so glad to see the rest of the lads before.

But the flagon-bearer hadn't taken three steps inside the room before he realized that something was wrong. Very wrong. Terrifyingly wrong.

The vast room was much smokier than he remembered. Warm, white tendrils of smoke were snaking across the floor, winding themselves around Stefan's legs and swirling up towards his face.

Surely the room had not been as hot as this either? After the cold stairway, the vast hall felt oppressive.

Stefan rubbed his eyes to peer through the smoke towards the fireplace. He could see now that there was only one figure, standing with its back towards him. Of the lads he had left behind, there was no sign. A cold trickle of fear ran down the boy's back. There was an odd silence in the room.

From the fireplace, Duncan spoke.

"Ah, Stefan Stinkle," he said in a voice that was deep and somehow dreadful,

"I wonder how much you have guessed of what has happened here today?"

Stefan found himself unable to answer, but his eyes must have shown that he understood only too well.

"Yes," said Duncan, "there are only three outcomes if a human meets a dragon. The human may kill the dragon. The dragon may kill the human. Or..."

Stefan found his voice. "Or the human becomes a dragon in human form," he whispered. "I didn't know... I mean I didn't..."

"Didn't you?" hissed Duncan. "Oh, I think you did, Stefan. As soon as I saw you, I knew what a very fine dragon you would make—you with your jealousy of everyone else, you with your interest in fame and treasure, you with your cold, cold heart. Will you really miss those other lads, do you think?"

"No," said Stefan Stinkle, and his cold heart became even colder.

"Welcome to the dragon world," said Duncan, and the smoke swirled up to hide the figure in the doorway.

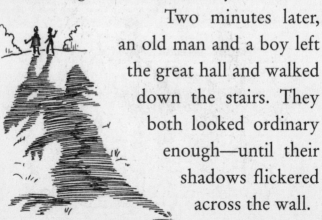

Two minutes later, an old man and a boy left the great hall and walked down the stairs. They both looked ordinary enough—until their shadows flickered across the wall.

Treasure
Trouble

Dragons love to collect treasure. It is one of their main pleasures in life. There is nothing a dragon loves more than to see a huge pile of treasure glinting and gleaming in the light of his fiery breath. Gold, silver and jewels are the most prized possessions. A dragon learns at an early age to detect fakes and cast them aside. Indeed, many a prince has been mortally offended to find that a dragon has raided his treasure-house and *left some things behind.* Dragons are some of the most discerning thieves in the world. At least, most of them are...

Not so long ago, a young dragon called Mildu was sent by his mother to his uncle to learn about the right way to go about acquiring treasure. Uncle Walpu was only too happy to put his nephew through his paces. His own collection of treasure was second to none.

The first part of the teaching was on the theory of treasure-seeking. Uncle Walpu dealt with methods of gaining entry into vaults, dungeons, banks and strongrooms. He explained how locks could be opened with claws and teeth or, failing that, by melting with a dragon's breath. Mildu proved an eager pupil.

Next, Uncle Walpu talked about the safest ways to carry treasure away. This can be tricky for a flying dragon, but wherever possible, dragons find a bag or net to put the treasure in. Mildu made practice flights holding rocks and branches, until he was quite confident.

"Remember," said Uncle Walpu, "if it's a choice between taking treasure or being able to make a safe getaway, leave the treasure behind. You can always go back for it another time. It really is better to be safe than sorry."

Mildu nodded wisely. There were a few more practice runs, in which the young dragon had to decide how much to carry. Finally, Uncle Walpu declared that he was satisfied. It was time for his nephew to go out on his first raid.

"There's a castle near here where a miserly old duke keeps a hoard of gold," said Uncle Walpu. "It's easy to get in and out, and the old man is too mean to keep many security people to protect all his property. You shouldn't have any trouble. Keep your wits about you, and bring back something nice for me, too!"

Mildu flew off, feeling nervous and excited. Back in his cave, Uncle Walpu paced up and down. He hoped that the young dragon would be successful this first time. He didn't want his confidence to be damaged. The mission should really pose no problems, but one never knew with a young dragon. They could lose their heads in a crisis.

But Uncle Walpu need not have worried. Within an hour, Mildu was back, carrying in his claws a big bag bulging with treasure. Uncle Walpu's eyes shone as he greeted his nephew.

"Any problems, lad?" he asked.

"It was easy," said Mildu. "Everything was in a big building outside the castle. I didn't have to go anywhere near the duke himself. And just look what I've got!"

Saying this, Mildu opened the big bag he had dumped on the floor. Uncle Walpu looked eagerly at the shining objects that clattered and spun on the floor of the cave. He couldn't believe his eyes.

"Mildu!" he cried, "what have you done? These are ... these are... *hub caps!*"

It was true. Rolling around the floor were twenty shiny hub caps. Rolls Royce hub caps. Mercedes hub caps. But hub caps all the same.

"Why," asked Uncle Walpu faintly, "did you bring these?"

"They're shiny," said Mildu. "Aren't they treasure, then?"

Uncle Walpu counted to eighty. He reflected that he had clearly missed out on teaching young Mildu some of the basics. It was back to theory for them both. It had never occurred to the older dragon that his nephew would need to be taught to recognize treasure when he saw it.

Three weeks later, after an intense course on hallmarks and gems, Uncle

Walpu felt that Mildu was ready once more. He had taught him all he knew about jewels, gold and silver. Surely, now, the lad was ready.

Once again, Mildu flew off, this time at night, to the castle with the miserly duke and the fleet of unused cars. Sadly, things did not go according to plan. The theft of the hub caps had, of course, been discovered. The duke, fearing quite rightly that the liberating of hub caps might be followed by the theft of something a good deal more valuable, updated his security system. He now had half a dozen men with dogs patrolling the grounds, while a

state-of-the-art alarm system was installed in the castle itself.

Now alarm systems, even state-of-the-art ones, do not usually assume that break-ins are going to happen from the air. Mildu landed on the roof without being detected. A little breathing on the lead of the roof, and Mildu had made a hole large enough for any dragon to get through. He clambered into the attics of the castle.

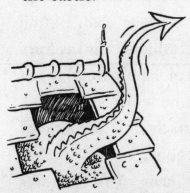

Mildu's plan had been to sneak all the way down the main stairs to the cellars, where he understood that most of the gold and silver was stored. It had not occurred to him that there would be anything worth stealing in the attics. But Mildu was surprised to see lots of square, shiny things stacked in a corner. He didn't know that these were gilded picture frames, or that the very odd-looking pictures of old-fashioned people in the middle were old masters and very valuable. He was simply taken by the shininess of the frames. Yes, Uncle Walpu had schooled Mildu long and carefully that all that glitters is not gold. He had instructed the young dragon always to look for a hallmark and, if possible, a maker's mark as well. But all this went right out of Mildu's head as soon as he saw such big golden objects. He felt sure that they must be worth something. And they weren't attached to any kind of car, so that must be good.

Mildu tied as many of the pictures as he could together with some rope he found in a corner. Then, clutching the rope with his claws, he launched himself

from the hole in the roof.
Unfortunately, the young
Mildu's rope-tying skills
were about as good as his
treasure-recognition skills.
As he flew over the castle
courtyard, one of the smaller paintings
slipped from the bundle and fell down,
down, down to the flagstones below. As
the picture passed the topmost windows
of the castle, the famous state-of-the-art
alarm sensors were triggered. A horrid
noise of bells and sirens filled the
air, frightening poor Mildu
half out of his wits.
A second later, he was
caught in the glare of
dozens of powerful
searchlights criss-
crossing the
grounds.

Now security men and women are used to some pretty strange sights, but a flying dragon is not one of them. They stood, open-mouthed, looking up at the apparition above them. The duke himself came running out of the castle and looked up as well. Coming as he did from a long

line of dragon-fighters (admittedly a very long time ago), he was less stunned by the sight than the security personnel.

"Shoot it!" he cried.

Mildu had no idea what this meant but he recognized a mean and vicious voice when he heard it. He pulled himself together and remembered Uncle Walpu's words. Dropping the bundle of pictures, he headed off towards the mountains as fast as his wings could carry him. The big pile of pictures, dropping like a stone, hit the unfortunate duke squarely on the head, putting an end to his miserly days and not doing a lot of good to the pictures in the process.

Back at his cave, Uncle Walpu was almost knocked off his feet by Mildu's hurried and inelegant landing. He didn't need to be told that things had gone badly wrong for his nephew.

It took Mildu some time to pant out his story. It took Uncle Walpu even longer to work out what had really happened, for Mildu knew nothing about searchlights and talked about monsters with big eyes instead. He didn't understand about alarm bells either, but said that the monsters had horrible shrill voices that shouted.

From all the confusion, Uncle Walpu picked out what was, to him, the only important point.

"What you stole, or tried to steal, Mildu," he said severely, "were pictures. Look at me, now. Are they on the list I made for you of the ten most desirable items of treasure?"

"No," said Mildu miserably.

"Are they even on my list of the hundred most desirable items of treasure?"

"No."

"So why did you steal … try to steal them then?"

"They were shiny," said Mildu, hanging his head.

Uncle Walpu completely lost his temper. "Windows are shiny!" he roared. "Bald heads are shiny! But should you try to steal them? NO! It is so simple, Mildu, that even a human could understand it. Gold, silver and jewels. Silver, gold and jewels. Gold, jewels and silver. It doesn't matter which way round you say it. There are only three things worth stealing. What are they?"

"Sold, jilder and gewels," said Mildu unhappily. At which his uncle gave a sigh that set fire to several trees three miles away and flapped off into the night to cool his temper in the moonlight.

It was clear that returning to the castle would not be a good idea. When he felt calmer, Uncle Walpu sat down and wrote out a plan for his nephew's further education. It was very detailed. It included lots of time for repetition and revision. It covered things so basic that most dragons would have been ashamed to have them pointed out. It was at just the right level, however, for Mildu. Uncle Walpu vowed to stay as calm as he could and prepared to do his duty.

Frankly, it was hopeless. Mildu appeared to grasp everything in a classroom situation, but as soon as he tried to put the theory into practice, things went disastrously wrong. His attempt to steal a shiny weather vane demolished the tower of a local church. His visit to a local bank left him locked into the vaults, from which he was rescued in the nick of time by Uncle Walpu. When he attempted to raid a jeweller's shop, he returned home with five huge imitation ingots made of plastic, which unfortunately had huge imitation plastic hallmarks on them.

After each disaster, Uncle Walpu took a few days off to regain his shattered composure. During these times, Mildu wandered idly around the mountainside, paddling in the cold, clear streams and amusing himself by kicking the rocks to create small avalanches. When one of these avalanches threatened to block up the entrance to Uncle Walpu's cave, while Uncle Walpu was inside it, Mildu was told not to go outside until he was given strict instructions on how to behave. The young dragon wandered around the network of caves instead, kicking at the walls and sighing heavily.

Uncle Walpu persevered for six months. He did everything he could. He even flew himself on treasure-seeking missions with Mildu, despite the fact that it is an unwritten dragon law that two dragons do not fly around together. After all, a human being might persuade himself that he was hallucinating if he saw one dragon in the sky, but two dragons take a lot more explaining.

Of course, side by side with his uncle, and with his uncle's voice talking him through every step, Mildu was fine. He could steal even the trickiest items when he had that kind of support. The problems came when the young dragon was let out on his own. Without some kind of guidance, Mildu went to pieces. He didn't think. He didn't plan. He didn't use his head at all. He had a fatal weakness for anything shiny, however unsuitable it was. At long last, even Uncle Walpu, who prided himself on his teaching skills, had to admit defeat.

"Mildu," he said, "I am going to send you back to your mother. It breaks my heart to let her down, for she has been relying on me to teach you all I know. But I must draw the line somewhere. I've spent so much time with you in the last few months that my own treasure-store has hardly grown at all. I've done all that I can for you. I'm afraid that you will never have treasure of your own and that is the end of it."

Mildu hung his head.

"I'm sorry," he said. "I have really tried hard. I guess I simply can't get all these difficult techniques into my head. I just can't understand why gold and silver and jewels found the easy way don't count as treasure."

"What are you talking about?" asked Uncle Walpu wearily. "What easy way is there?"

"Why, collecting the treasure that is just sitting in the mountains, waiting to be found, of course," said Mildu. "Look, I'll show you!"

He led his uncle deep into the cave and kicked at a wall. Several glittering objects fell to the ground or sparkled in the wall. They were diamonds! Outside, Mildu showed his uncle the little nuggets of gold he had found in the streams and piled up behind a convenient rock.

For several moments, Uncle Walpu was speechless. Then he smiled.

"If I was wearing a hat, I would take it off to you, young Mildu," he said. "Of course this is real treasure, and why we dragons go flying about risking burglar alarms and guards with guns when all this is here, I can't imagine. I really don't have anything left to teach you. Tell your mother she should be proud of you and go straight home."

"Couldn't I just stay a few more days?" asked Mildu.

"Certainly not!" laughed Uncle Walpu. "The diamonds and gold on this mountain are *mine*!"

The Flightless Dragon

Many baby birds have to be taught how to fly by their parents. If they are reluctant, a little push from a high branch usually does the trick. The little birds start flapping by instinct and before they know what they are doing, they're flying! If only it was as simple as that for baby dragons...

Many a dragon mother has, I'm sure, been tempted to take her offspring up the mountain to a handy precipice and give him a hearty shove. Unfortunately, with dragons, it's just too big a risk to take. Dragons are not light and feathery, like birds. They are large and scaly. They need to develop considerable strength in their wings and shoulders before they can fly. If you pushed a baby dragon off the top of a mountain, I'm afraid there would not be much of him left to be scraped up in the valley below.

Almost as soon as they have hatched, little dragons are given exercises to do by their mothers. That is exactly what happened to Plodlu.

"*Rotate* those shoulders!" called his mother. "Let me see your muscles working, Plodlu! One, two, three, four! *And* the other way. Four, three, two, one! And *up*! And *down*! Now one more time!"

Poor Plodlu was not an athletic young dragon. He was a sitting-down-by-the-fire kind of dragon. He didn't take naturally to all this effort. But he did wiggle his shoulders a little to show willing and tried to copy his mother.

After several days of these special strengthening exercises, Plodlu's mother moved on to wing extensions.

"*Stretch* those wings!" she cried. "Out, in, out, in … *all* the way, Plodlu! Well, move away from the wall then! Now, again! One, two, out, in, three, four, out, in!"

Once again, Plodlu struggled, but he could tell by his mother's tone of voice that this was important, so he did his best.

A few weeks later, Plodlu's mother took him outside and made him jump up and down while flapping his wings.

"Feel that lift!" she shouted, landing rather heavily herself. "Up, down, up, down, that's the way! Not too near the edge now!"

Plodlu tried to feel the lift but all he really felt was silly. Here he was, a plump and rather clumsy young dragon, heaving himself up and down like a forkful of mashed potato. He couldn't get the wing and jump sequence right for a start. He was always lifting his wings as he jumped, which his mother said was wrong.

"No, no, no!" she yelled. "*Down* with the wings and *up* with the legs. Stop, stop! That's not right. Now, legs first. Up, down, up, down. Now add the wings … down, up, down, up. Oh dear. All right, pick yourself up and let's start again."

Plodlu's mother hadn't expected to be doing quite so much exercise herself while teaching her little one to fly. But while she got fitter and fitter, Plodlu got more and more confused. Pretty soon, his mother had him doing practice take-offs along a broad, flat ledge on the mountainside. He had to run along, flapping his wings and getting faster and faster until, for a few short steps, he was gliding through the air.

"Faster, Plodlu! Faster!" cried his mother, thundering along behind. "Don't forget to flap!"

But Plodlu simply couldn't do both things at once. If he remembered to run faster (and it seemed that acceleration was pretty important), then he forgot to flap his wings. If he remembered the flapping, he simply jogged along at a pace that wouldn't have got a feather into the air, let alone a rather solid dragon. Plodlu's mother tried to think of enticements.

Next morning, when Plodlu woke and wanted his breakfast, his mother smiled and said, "Well, it's up on that big rock at the end of the ledge. Run along, flapping, and you'll be able to jump up and get it."

Plodlu loved his breakfast. He went outside and began trotting along the ledge with rather more enthusiasm than he had

before. But he found that thoughts of his waiting breakfast put him off completely. He couldn't flap and run and think about breakfast at the same time. In fact, he couldn't do anything and think about breakfast at the same time. Thirty seconds later, Plodlu's mother heard a plaintive cry and came out to find her son clinging by his claw-tips to the edge of the ledge. His acceleration had improved, but his sense of direction hadn't.

After that, Plodlu was too frightened to try running along the ledge again. His mother took him up to the top of the mountain, where there was a flat, grassy plateau, just right for a learner.

Plodlu ran and ran and ran. But no matter how much flapping he did, he didn't take off.

"It's co-ordination again," sighed his mother. "If only you had a little more sense of *rhythm*, Plodlu. Just a minute, I've got it!"

Plodlu's mother stomped off and came back with a very old wind-up gramophone that she had liberated from a wealthy duke some years before. She wound the turntable and heard the sounds of a delightful waltz wafting across the plateau.

"There you are, Plodlu!" she cried. "Just copy me!"

And with a *one, two, three, one, two, three, one, two, three*, she was off, whirling and twirling, sometimes on the ground and sometimes in the air. It looked pretty good.

Plodlu listened hard to the music. He set off, feet flying and wings flapping, around and around and around … until he was sick. His mother turned off the music with a sigh and carried him home. Clearly, more work needed to be done.

Over the next few weeks, Plodlu's mother showed a great deal of inventiveness. She made him several exercise machines from branches and rocks she found lying about. Using this equipment, Plodlu did find himself getting stronger. He lifted his dumb-bells, practised his sit-ups, and stepped up and down on to several big rocks until he could lift, sit and step no more. Even his mother was impressed.

"You're shaping up nicely, Plodlu," she said. "Now all we have to do is to put your exercises into practice. It's time for some real flying. You have the strength now, you simply have to learn the skill."

Plodlu felt a lot more confident with his new muscles. He even skipped along as his mother led him to a grassy slope on the other side of the mountain.

"Now," she said, "all you have to do is to run down the slope, flapping as hard u can, and you'll soon find yourself the air."

Plodlu looked down at the slope. It was fairly steep but there was no horrible precipice at the other end. He took a deep breath, stretched out his wings, and set off. Faster and faster, Plodlu flapped and ran. His little legs twinkled along the ground. His little wings could hardly be seen, they moved so fast. Halfway down the slope, could it be? *Yes!* Plodlu had taken off! He was flying! Er … no, wait, what…? Plodlu's mother rubbed her eyes. What on earth was the boy doing? He couldn't be, could he? As Plodlu swung around towards her, she was sure. *He was flying upside down!*

Plodlu's mother sat down on the grass and hid her eyes. She had never, ever heard of a dragon flying upside down. It could only end in disaster. It did.

Plodlu, unable to judge the steepness of the slope, crash landed. Naturally, as he had been flying upside down, he crash landed on his head. A dazed and confused young dragon lay on the grass.

"Plodlu, sweetheart, are you all right?" cried his mother, bending over him tenderly.

"Lollipops," said Plodlu distinctly. "Lollipops and gravy."

Clearly, he was suffering from serious concussion if not something worse. Plodlu's mother gently carried him home and put him to bed in their cave. It was several days before the young dragon was himself again, and even then he had a lump on his head that took weeks to go away. It seemed cruel to pursue the flying lessons when he was poorly.

While she looked after Plodlu, his mother had time to think. Would her son

always be so hopeless at flying? What would be the best way of keeping him safe in the future? The more she thought about it, the more the older dragon was forced to come to the conclusion that the safest thing would be if Plodlu never flew again.

A dragon who cannot fly? A flightless dragon? Plodlu's mother turned these phrases over in her mind and felt deeply uneasy. She had never heard of a dragon who could not fly. Her Great-Uncle Nobu, who lived a long way to the east, had injured his left wing once. It never was any good for flying after that. But Great-Uncle Nobu had managed very well with only one wing. For a long time, he could only fly in circles, but after a while, even that was sorted out. But not flying at all? That was a different matter, and one that worried Plodlu's mother a great deal. Night after night, she sat by her son's bedside and worried.

As it turned out, Plodlu's mother was worrying about the wrong thing. As soon as Plodlu was better again, he was eager to get back into the air.

"It was great, Mum," he said. "I really enjoyed the flying. I don't know why I went upside down. It just sort of happened. What I need is more practice."

Reluctantly, his mother took him out to the grassy slope once more. This time, she covered the slope with leaves and hay so that if (she thought it was more likely to be *when*) Plodlu came heavily to earth, his landing would be cushioned. She was right. Plodlu crashed several more times, each time hurting a different part of his body. In the process, he perfected upside-down flying, sideways flying, loop-the-looping and sky-diving. He looked remarkably graceful in the air. It was just the landings that were lacking.

"Perhaps if I landed on water," he mused one day.

His mother was horrified.

"No, Plodlu!" she cried. "You know perfectly well that water and dragons don't mix. If you manage to put your flames out, it will be no end of trouble to light them again. It's too big a risk to take."

Even Plodlu could see the sense of this. But he really didn't like crashing into the ground quite so often. Then, one evening, he had a brainwave.

"I've got it!" he told his mother. "I know how to stop hurting myself!"

"Practising your landings?" asked his mother. "Or giving up flying entirely?" These days, after nursing Plodlu through two broken legs, a badly twisted elbow and a dislocated knee, she was open to any suggestion. But she was not ready for what Plodlu said next.

"If I stay up in the air all the time, there won't be a problem," he said airily. "My difficulty is landing. The solution is not to land. I'm surprised I didn't think of it before."

"But…" said his mother. "I mean, how…? I mean, that's ridiculous! You can't just stay up there! You'll get tired!"

"Not if I glide," said Plodlu. "I can stay up for ever if I just glide and rest. I can even sleep when I'm gliding. I had a

little go this morning. The thermals around the top of the mountain are really strong. There's no danger at all."

"What about food?" asked his mother faintly. "There isn't anything to eat up there, unless you're going to start munching birds, and I've never fancied feathers, myself. Surely you're not going to do that, Plodlu? You'll need to eat to keep up your strength, sweetheart!"

"You could throw my meals up to me," said Plodlu calmly. "I'm so good at aerial acrobatics now, I wouldn't have any trouble in catching them. Then, when I'm a bit older, I'll practise seizing maidens on the wing. It should be pretty easy with the element of surprise. By the time they know what's happening, the silly things will be breakfast."

"But what are you going to do all day?" asked the poor mother dragon. "Won't you get bored, just flying around?"

For Plodlu's mother, flying was a purely practical matter. A dragon flew, she thought, in order to get from A to B. She didn't understand the pleasure her son got from gliding and zooming, twizzling and turning. It all seemed very strange to her.

Plodlu was laughing. "I won't be bored at all," he chuckled. "I'll be so busy building up my business, I won't have time to wonder what to do."

"Business?" Plodlu's mother felt she had come into the plot several pages too late and couldn't grasp what was going on.

"Yes," said her son confidently. "I'm going to run a dragon aerial acrobatic show. We should get lots of spectators. And they may like to pay in food, too, you never know."

"But there are only a handful of dragons for miles around," said Plodlu's mother. "You'd only ever have an audience of about three, although I, of course, will always come and watch you."

"Not dragons," explained Plodlu, "*humans*! They're the ones with spare maidens to eat and buns to throw."

At this point, Plodlu's mother, who had been feeling faint for some time, fell with a crash to the ground. This time it was Plodlu who had to do the looking after for a while. He knew why his mother was worried. Dragons and humans have not, traditionally, got on well together. Dragons profess not to understand this. It doesn't seem to occur to them that visits involving stealing treasure and munching maidens are not occasions of joy for the human world. Humans have no particular interest in seeing the better side of dragons either. They have several excellent legends about heroes who have bravely slain any dragon who crossed their paths. It would be unfortunate if they ever found out that most dragons are pussy-cats underneath. They are gentle, kind, funny and friendly (but they do enjoy the odd maiden for breakfast, it's true).

Plodlu's mother did her best to talk him out of his plan, but he had made up his mind. Perhaps you have heard of the flying dragons of China? The rolling dragons of Afghanistan? The tumbling dragons of Japan? The cloud dragons of Peru? They are all a single dragon, of course—our old friend Plodlu. And where

Plodlu goes, his poor old mother is sure to be found skulking behind a nearby hill.

So that is how a dragon with very poor flying skills, who looked at one point as though he would never fly in his life, became the famous flying dragon we all hear so much about. It just goes to show what determination can do for you, but I wouldn't advise that you try it at home yourself. We simply don't have the wings for it.

The Dragon's Egg

Wizard Wazoo was in trouble. In fact, he was in the deepest trouble of his terribly troubled life. Ever since he was a small wizard, learning at his father's knee, he had made mistakes. A mistake in your maths homework can be a problem. It may incur the wrath of your teacher or your parents, but it doesn't turn them blue or make your house dissolve. Wizard Wazoo's mistakes did things just like that. It was very fortunate that his father was a wizard as well, because most of the time

he could put things right without too much trouble. Sadly, the older wizard is no longer waving his wand in our world. These days, Wizard Wazoo is on his own. So these days, Wizard Wazoo is in trouble more often than he is out of it. And even his cat, Carlaminda, can't help him.

The particularly bad trouble that I mentioned at the beginning of this story came about because Wizard Wazoo was fond of strawberries. Being a wizard, he didn't see why he should have to wait until summer to enjoy his favourite fruit. A little bit of wand-waving here, a sprinkling of magic dust there, and *hey presto!* … straw. Ooops.

As is often the way, what had started as a mild wish for strawberries became desperate as soon as there was difficulty in obtaining them. Wizard Wazoo fixed his wizard stare on the pile of

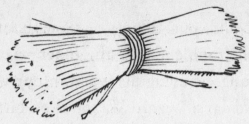

straw. He clenched his wizard teeth and muttered his wizard words. *Da DA!* In a second the straw turned into a pile of cranberries.

Cranberries are all very well in their way. They make a refreshing drink. They go well with turkey. But they don't do anything for a wizard with a requirement for strawberries. Wizard Wazoo rolled up his sleeves. He got out his most powerful wand. He cleaned out his second-best cauldron and started to make a berry-bringing brew. It contained snails, slug-

slime, used tea-bags, peppermint foot lotion, orange peel and one or two other ingredients that you would probably prefer not to know about. Wizard Wazoo stirred and murmured. Carlaminda, seeing the green steam rising steadily from the cauldron, ran under the bed and stayed there with her head in her paws.

Soon, the green steam turned to blue steam. The smell became very bad indeed. The bubbling of the mixture seemed to take on a life of its own. Wizard Wazoo looked back at his spell book, its most popular pages spattered with past potions. He checked his ingredients, read the instructions, turned over two pages at once, and made the fateful mistake of saying the magic words backwards.

There was silence for a long moment, during which the only sounds were the sluggish bubbling of the mixture and the whimpering of Carlaminda, who had a pretty good idea of what was going to happen next. Suddenly, it was as if three brass bands and a road-drill had squeezed into the room at once. Everything that could clatter clattered. Everything that could bong bonged. The glasses tinkled. The windows twinkled (loudly). Wizard Wazoo's teeth chattered and he had a very strange feeling, as if someone was trying to turn him inside out. Then there was a puff of orange smoke, a clash of cymbals (or possibly saucepan lids) and the house zoomed into the air and headed for Siberia.

Wizard Wazoo shut his eyes until the house landed. He didn't have to look out of the window to know that it was very, very cold. Shivering and shaking, he relit his fire and pulled his cloak around him. He had to work out how to get home. And the worse thing of all was that his craving for strawberries had not stayed at home. If there was one single thing that Wizard Wazoo knew about Siberia, it was that strawberries were remarkably thin on the ground.

Five hours later, although the fire was roaring under his second-best cauldron, Wizard Wazoo had icicles growing from his toes. He found it terribly hard to concentrate on his spell book when he felt so cold. He had skimmed through all the easier spells at the beginning of the book, hoping to find something he could adapt. Nothing was suitable. Even the fairly-hard spells in the middle of the book, which Wizard Wazoo only attempted on his better days, were no use. The freezing wizard was forced to look at the very difficult spells towards the end.

The last section of the book had pristine white pages that had never been touched by a wizard's potion-spattered fingers. They advised on many problems that Wizard Wazoo hadn't even known existed. His eyes opened wider and wider at each page he turned. "How to tame a wild brontosaurus" had three pages of ingredients and such a complicated set of instructions that Wizard Wazoo couldn't even understand the first one. "How to open the packaging on supermarket cheese sandwiches" seemed to require a level of wizardry that Wizard Wazoo had no hope of ever acquiring.

The poor wizard, whose feet felt like ice and whose fingers really *were* ice by now, had almost given up hope when he turned the last page and saw "How to send your house back home from Siberia and find strawberries at the same time."

With mounting excitement, Wizard Wazoo read through the list of ingredients. Toenail clippings—yes! Marmalade—yes! Cucumber face cream and a pink sponge— yes! Lawnmower oil—yes! Sixteen-day-old pea soup—strangely enough, yes! Two holly leaves—yes! The longest quill of a bad-tempered porcupine—yes! Three jars of pickled onions—yes, yes, yes! A dragon's egg—oh... It was the very last ingredient, and poor Wizard Wazoo knew perfectly well that he didn't have one. He looked vaguely around the frosty room, but he knew it was hopeless. Dragon's eggs are big. They're not the kind of thing you could miss. Wizard Wazoo crouched over his fire and tried to think.

At that moment, Carlaminda, who felt she couldn't bear to stay in Siberia a moment longer than was necessary, crawled out from under the bed and curled around Wizard Wazoo's all-too spindly and shivering legs. She pointed her pretty paw delicately at the word "dragon" and waved elegantly at the window. Wizard Wazoo looked at her blankly.

Carlaminda gave a sigh of deep-felt exasperation and hurried over to the book shelf. She pulled down a magazine with her teeth and carried it over to her master. Wizard Wazoo looked down at the brightly coloured cover. "A new magic cloak in a weekend!" he read. "My wife's a warlock!" screamed the cover. "Free with this issue two packets of super spells!" it went on. "Siberia: undiscovered land of magic and mystery!" it finished, and there was a picture of a smiling dragon sliding down a snowy slope and waving at the reader with both hands.

Wizard Wazoo peered at the picture. Then he tried to open the magazine to read the story inside. It wasn't easy with frozen fingers, but at last he found the page. It seemed that Siberia was trying to attract more holidaymakers and had decided to target the readers of *Magic Monthly*. One of the attractions, he read, as well as the bracing climate and the soothing scenery, was the Drooski Dragon Park, where real live dragons could be seen in their natural environment.

In no time at all, Wizard Wazoo had pulled on his extra-thick hiking socks, wrapped his neck in a moth-eaten scarf, and pulled his wizard's staff from the pot where it had been holding up an unhealthy looking plant. He threw open the door, letting in blasts of snow and frozen air, and plunged out into the wintery wilderness beyond. Then he hesitated, staggered back into the room, picked up a protesting and squirming Carlaminda and tucked her under his cloak.

The conditions outside were truly atrocious. Wizard Wazoo hunched his shoulders and tried to think himself warmer. In this he was, surprisingly, quite successful, although Carlaminda doing her own magic under the cloak may well have helped a good deal.

Gradually, as the wizard struggled on, the weather improved. The blizzard stopped and the sun came out, almost blinding Wazoo with its brilliance. It was hard to know which way to go, but as luck would have it (and Wizard Wazoo was not renowned for his acquaintance with luck) he spotted a large sign ahead. "Welcome," it said, "to the Drooski Dragon Park. Entrance: 12,000 roubles."

Poor old Wizard Wazoo didn't have one rouble, never mind 12,000. He was about to sink down into the snow in despair when he realized that there was no one at the gate to take his money. He had happened to turn up at just the moment when the gatekeeper went off to have his seven-hour lunch. Feeling slightly guilty, Wizard Wazoo slipped through the gates and into the park, picking up a leaflet from an open box as he did so.

Wizard Wazoo had (temporarily) learnt his lesson as far as reading useful instructions was concerned. He stopped and conscientiously read what the leaflet

had to say about not feeding the dragons and trying not to disturb them when they were sleeping. There was also a section entitled: "Safety Note". It was not very encouraging. "If attacked by a dragon," it said, "try screaming. If that doesn't work, you will have nothing more to worry about ... ever."

For the first time, it occurred to Wizard Wazoo that he should have brought his book of spells with him. It also crossed his mind that perhaps mother dragons were not madly keen on complete strangers coming and stealing their eggs. Thirdly, it came to Wizard Wazoo that a dragon's egg, as well as being large, might be very heavy. Could he remember enough magic to get it back to his snow-bound house? Wizard Wazoo was not much of a wizard at the best of times. Now, he felt every simple carrying spell he had ever known slip silently out of his head. All I need now, he thought glumly, is to meet an irritable dragon.

"Ahem!" A voice behind him made the wizard wheel around like a Cossack dancer. His worst nightmare had come true. Standing before him, not six feet away, was the biggest dragon he had ever seen. In truth, he had never seen one at all in the flesh before, and he found now that magazines gave an entirely misleading impression of their size. And this dragon didn't just look irritable. She looked out and out *furious*.

"About time too!" said the dragon in fluent Wizard. "Come on, come on, let's not hang around here. It's freezing. Even with my fire-breathing, I find this climate intensely annoying. Are you coming or not? Well?"

Wizard Wazoo looked bemused. "What?" he stuttered. "Where?"

"To find an egg, of course," said the dragon crossly. "I don't have one myself at the moment, but my neighbour is terribly careless with hers. She won't even notice if we borrow one."

As if in a trance, poor Wizard Wazoo followed the dragon through the snow. When they came to a hillside, she told him to wait and disappeared into a cave. A couple of minutes later, she emerged, holding something that looked like a very large boulder.

"I can't carry that!" cried Wizard Wazoo. "I couldn't even lift it. Oh no, whatever am I going to do? I wish I hadn't ever said that spell this morning. Why didn't I listen to everything my poor old father told me? I'm a total failure as a wizard. Oh dear!"

"Have you quite finished?" asked the dragon coldly. "You don't have to carry the egg, do you? I'm doing that. And as for the rest, it's past caring for."

She stomped off across the snow with the egg, pausing only to check that Wizard Wazoo was following her. Inside the wizard's cloak, Carlaminda kept very still. She had an uncomfortable feeling that she might make a tasty snack for a dragon.

When the unlikely pair reached the wizard's house, now almost covered with snow, the dragon gave a big sigh.

"This place is hopelessly small," she said. "Do something about it, will you?"

Wizard Wazoo gaped. "M-m-make it bigger, you mean?" he asked.

"Well, I certainly don't want to be smaller," said the dragon witheringly. "Come on. It's a pretty simple spell, I believe. Round about page 18 of your spell book, I think."

The wizard almost panicked, but just in the nick of time, the spell came floating into his mind. A few swift words and a tap on the door with his wizard's staff, and the house kind of shook itself and grew to about double its previous size. It was still a bit of a squeeze for the dragon to fit through the door, but she squeezed in and dumped the egg on the floor.

"Come on," she said, "get on with the spell, will you?"

"You're coming, too?" asked Wazoo, trying and failing to imagine the dragon in the quiet suburb where he lived.

"Of course," said the dragon.

On reflection, Wizard Wazoo realized that there was absolutely nothing he could do about it. He concentrated on the spell instead. It certainly taxed all his powers. Once or twice he felt sure that he had gone wrong, but at last all the steps were done and it only remained for the final word to be said. Wizard Wazoo said it.

In a flash, a breeze of warm air wrapped around the house. There was a shaking and a sound of breaking. Then the house, still much larger, was back in Wizard Wazoo's garden. And on every surface there was a large bowl of strawberries.

"But why did you help me?" asked a relieved Wizard Wazoo, gazing in wonder at the dragon.

"For the strawberries, of course," she said. "Take your hands off that bowl right now!"